# Oliver Twist

**by**
**Charles Dickens**

adapted by
Marian Leighton

Illustrations by
Ric Estrada

MOBY BOOKS

PLAYMORE, INC., Publishers
Under arrangement with I. WALDMAN & SON, INC.
New York, New York

# ILLUSTRATED CLASSIC EDITIONS

edited by

Malvina G. Vogel

Copyright © 1979 by

I. WALDMAN & SON, INC.
New York, New York
All rights reserved

# Contents

# About the Author

Charles Dickens was born in Landport, Portsea, England, in 1812, the second of eight children. His father, a clerk, moved the family to London when Charles was ten years old. Two years later, the boy had to leave school to help support the family.

But Charles read constantly in his spare time. He also wandered around the poor working-class districts and the slum areas where criminals hung out. These places and their inhabitants were described vividly in his novels.

In 1832, Dickens, who had since returned to school, became a newspaper reporter. Four years later, he published *Pickwick Papers*, his first major novel. *Oliver Twist* appeared in 1838. Other leading works included *David Copperfield*, *A Christmas Carol*, *Great Expectations*, and *A Tale of Two Cities*.

# People You Will Read About

Oliver Twist, *a poor orphan who seems destined for a life of misery and crime*

Mr. Bumble, *the greedy parish official in charge of the workhouse where Oliver is raised*

Mrs. Corney, *the workhouse matron who learns the secret of Oliver's true identity*

Mr. Sowerberry, *the undertaker who takes Oliver in as his apprentice*

Noah Claypole, *the undertaker's assistant who makes life miserable for Oliver*

Fagin, *an old man who is the leader of a gang of thieves and housebreakers*

The Artful Dodger ⎱ *teen-age thieves in Fagin's*
Charley Bates ⎰ *gang*

Bill Sikes, *a thief and murderer, and Fagin's accomplice in crime*

Toby Crackit, *another of Fagin's accomplices who plans some of the gang's jobs*

Nancy, *a girl in Fagin's gang who tries to help Oliver*

Mr. Brownlow, *a kindly old gentleman who befriends Oliver and searches for his identity*

Mrs. Bedwin, *Mr. Brownlow's devoted housekeeper*

Mr. Grimwig, *Mr. Brownlow's friend who doubts Oliver's loyalty*

Monks, *the mysterious man with secret reasons for wanting to destroy Oliver*

Mrs. Maylie, *a gentle woman who takes Oliver into her home*

Rose Maylie, *a beautiful girl who befriends Oliver*

A Mother Dies in Childbirth.

# CHAPTER 1

# A Lonesome Childhood

In the workhouse of a parish in England, on a date long forgotten, a baby boy was born. His mother died in childbirth.

"The mother was so young and pretty! Who was she?" asked the doctor.

"I don't know," replied the nurse. "Someone found her lying in the street last night and brought her inside. She must have walked a long way because her shoes are all worn out. But no one knows where she came from."

"I guess she wasn't married," said the doctor. "There's no wedding ring on her finger." With that, the doctor left the baby in the care

9

of the workhouse people who looked after or-phans such as that baby who was named Oliver Twist.

Before he was a year old, Oliver was sent to another workhouse. He spent the next eight years there with 25 other children. Some were troublemakers and some, like Oliver, simply had no parents to take care of them. Mrs. Mann, who ran the workhouse, received money from the parish to buy food and clothes for the children. However, she kept most of the money for herself. The only time she bathed the children and gave them enough to eat was when an official from the parish church came to inspect the workhouse.

Such an inspection took place on Oliver's ninth birthday. The child was thin and pale and always hungry and unhappy. The parish official, Mr. Bumble, came to see Mrs. Mann about him. Mr. Bumble was a fat, middle-aged man with a bad temper.

"So Oliver Twist is nine years old today?"

Money for Food and Clothes

"Yes," replied Mrs. Mann.

"Do you know that the parish offered a big reward for information leading to his father or some other family member? We never discovered to whom he belongs."

"Where did he get the name Oliver Twist?" asked Mrs. Mann.

"I made it up myself," said Mr. Bumble. "I name all our orphans in alphabetical order. The one before him was 'S,' so I called him Swubble. This one was 'T,' so he was Twist. I have names picked out all the way to 'Z.'"

"Well, Mr. Bumble, why do you ask about Oliver today?"

"He is too old to stay here, Mrs. Mann. I have come to take him back to the workhouse where he was born."

So Oliver was given a slice of bread, then dressed in a simple outfit and a brown cloth cap. He followed Mr. Bumble to the new workhouse. There, Oliver was brought before a committee of ten men.

Off to Another Workhouse

"What's your name, boy?" growled the chairman of the committee.

"Oliver Twist, sir."

"I guess you know that you're an orphan."

"What's that, sir?"

"That means that you have no mother or father and have been raised by the parish."

Oliver began to cry.

"Stop crying!" ordered the chairman. "You should say your prayers and thank the good people of the church who feed you!"

"But I don't know how to pray."

"What you need, boy, is a good trade!"

Oliver cried himself to sleep that night on a hard, narrow bed. The next day, he had his first meal with the other children in the workhouse. Not only did the food taste terrible, but it never filled the children's stomachs. They had nothing but thin soup three times a day, with an onion twice a week and half a roll on Sundays. After three months of near-starvation, the children drew

"You're an Orphan."

lots to decide who would ask for a second helping. Oliver Twist was chosen.

Oliver picked up his empty bowl and went up to Mr. Limbkins, who was serving supper.

"Please, sir, may I have some more?" the boy whispered.

"What did you say?" roared Mr. Limbkins, who could hardly believe his ears.

"I would like some more supper."

Mr. Limbkins screamed for Mr. Bumble.

"That child will come to no good!" said Mr. Bumble. "Put him in a room by himself. That will teach him to ask for too much to eat!"

The next morning, Mr. Bumble posted a sign outside the workhouse. It offered a sum of five pounds to anyone who would take Oliver away and teach him a trade.

Oliver Asks For a Second Helping.

Mr. Gamfield Needs a Chimney Sweep.

# CHAPTER 2

# Learning a Trade

Mr. Bumble spanked Oliver every day with his cane. The poor boy couldn't wait to get away from the workhouse!

One day Mr. Gamfield, a chimney sweep, was walking by the workhouse. He saw the sign on the wall.

"I could teach this boy how to be a chimney sweep," he told Mr. Limbkins.

"That's a nasty job," Mr. Limbkins replied. "Young boys can smother in chimneys."

"You won't let me have him, then?"

"I'll give him to you for three pounds. It's a good deal. You won't have to spend much to take care of the boy—he's never had much to eat! And if he gives you any trouble, just spank him!"

Mr. Bumble asked the judge to sign papers transferring Oliver to Mr. Gamfield.

"You're going to be an apprentice, Oliver," Mr. Bumble explained.

"What's that, sir?"

"Mr. Gamfield is going to teach you a trade and make a man out of you."

Suddenly, the judge saw a look of great fear on Oliver's face and tears in his eyes.

"What's the matter?" asked the judge.

Oliver got down on his knees, sobbing bitterly. He begged the judge not to give him over to such a mean man as Mr. Gamfield. The judge tore up the papers and ordered Mr. Bumble to return Oliver to the workhouse and to treat him better.

Mr. Sowerberry, the undertaker, was the next man to read the sign on the workhouse wall. "I can use somebody to help me in my

Oliver Begs the Judge.

business of burying dead people," he thought. So Mr. Sowerberry called upon Mr. Bumble.

"Would you like to have the boy?" asked Mr. Bumble. "For five pounds, he's yours!"

Oliver gathered up his belongings, which were so few in number that they all fitted into one small paper bag. Then he went with Mr. Bumble to the undertaker's house. He cried all the way over there.

"What's wrong with you?" snapped Mr. Bumble. "You should be glad that the undertaker is giving you a home."

"I'm sorry, sir," mumbled Oliver, "but I'm so lonely. Nobody likes me. Please don't be mean to me!"

Mrs. Sowerberry, a short, plump woman with a wrinkled face, opened the door.

"He's so small," she said, looking at Oliver. "Looks like a bag of bones."

The undertaker's wife took Oliver into a cold little kitchen.

"Charlotte," she ordered the maid, "give

"He Looks Like a Bag of Bones."

this boy some of the cold meat that was put out for the dog!"

Anyone who could have seen the half-starved boy clutch at the strips of leftover meat would have been horrified. When Oliver had finished, Mrs. Sowerberry came for him.

"Come to your bed," she said. "It's under the counter among the coffins. Hurry along!"

Oliver's new room was even more lonely and frightening than the one at the work-house. All around him were coffins waiting for dead bodies to fill them. There were also wooden boards to build more coffins. Oliver slept on a hard mattress. The room was very dark and hot.

In the morning, someone kicked at the door.

"Do you need a coffin, sir?" Oliver asked.

"Shut up!" said a young man as he entered. "I'm Noah Claypole, and you'll be working under me."

Noah was a charity boy but not a work-

A Lonely, Frightening Place to Sleep

house orphan. He knew who his parents were, but they were too poor to take care of him.

Mr. Sowerberry showed Oliver what undertakers do. One day they went to the house of a woman who had just died. Her husband and children stood crying over the body. Mr. Sowerberry brought a coffin, and he and Noah carried the body to the churchyard and buried it. They asked Oliver if he would like to be an undertaker.

"No!" replied the boy firmly.

"Well, you'll get used to it," said Mr. Sowerberry. "You'll have to."

Oliver was badly treated by Mrs. Sowerberry and Charlotte, but especially by Noah. One day, Noah insulted Oliver's dead mother. The little boy, who looked too weak to swat a fly, grabbed Noah by the throat and shook him violently. Then he hurled him to the ground with a fierce blow.

"Oliver is going to kill me!" cried Noah.

Oliver Hurls Noah to the Ground.

"Help me, Charlotte! Help me, Mrs. Sowerberry! Get him off me!"

The two women dragged Oliver into the cold, dark cellar and locked the door.

"Go get Mr. Bumble!" Mrs. Sowerberry told Noah. "Tell him what Oliver did!"

"Mr. Bumble!" cried Noah upon reaching the workhouse. "Come quickly! Oliver. . . ."

"Ran away?" asked Mr. Bumble.

"No, sir, but he tried to kill me!"

"I knew that boy would come to no good!"

"Noah called my mother bad names," Oliver explained to Mr. Bumble when he reached the undertaker's house.

"She deserved it!" said Noah.

"That's a lie!" snapped the boy.

Mr. Sowerberry spanked Oliver and shut him in his room with nothing but a stale piece of bread. When the boy was alone, he let the tears fall. Later, in the middle of the night, he slipped softly out of the house forever.

Dragging Oliver off Noah

On His Way to London

# CHAPTER 3

# Fagin and His Boys

Oliver walked more than 70 miles. He carried only a shirt, two pairs of stockings, and a single penny. He was on his way to London! No one—not even Mr. Bumble—would ever find him in that big city. It was cold and his feet were sore, but he was thrilled to leave his old, unhappy life behind. He begged at cottages for food and water and slept in haystacks in the meadows.

On the seventh day of his journey, Oliver met a boy who looked about his own age, but who dressed and acted like a man. He was short and bow-legged and had ugly little eyes. He wore dirty clothes and a hat that looked about ready to fall off his head. His pants were baggy, and his coat reached down well below his knees.

"Hi, young fella!" he greeted Oliver. "What're ya up to?"

"I'm tired and hungry. I've been on the road for seven days," Oliver replied.

"Well, c'mon, I'll get ya some food."

Jack Dawkins, better known as the Artful Dodger, bought some ham and bread and then took Oliver to a tavern for some beer. It was the biggest meal Oliver had ever eaten.

"Going to London?" asked the Dodger.

"Yes," said Oliver.

"Got anywhere to stay?"

"No."

"Got any money?"

"No."

"Well, it just so happens that I'm going to London too, and I know a gentleman there who will give you free room and board if I

The Artful Dodger Offers Oliver Food.

introduce you."

The boys came to a filthy, bad-smelling street and entered a broken-down house.

"Are you there, Fagin?" called the Dodger. "I have a new pal for you!"

An ugly old man in a dirty flannel dressing gown was cooking sausages. He had matted red hair, and his face was twisted into an ugly grin. At a table in front of the fireplace sat four or five boys, none older than the Dodger, smoking long clay pipes and drinking spirits. The only furniture in the room was a clothes rack on which many silk handkerchiefs hung and some dirty sacks that were used as beds.

"This is my new friend, Oliver Twist," the Dodger announced.

Fagin glanced at Oliver, who looked bewildered. Then he drew out a box from a trap door in the floor. Inside were beautiful gold watches, bracelets, rings, and other jewelry.

"These pretty things are mine," said Fagin

Meeting Fagin and His Gang

nervously. "They are all I have left in my old age."

Oliver didn't understand why a man with so many riches lived in such a run-down house, but he decided that Fagin must spend all his money taking care of the boys.

Oliver washed himself in a basin and threw the dirty water out the window, as Fagin suggested. Then he ate breakfast with Fagin, the Dodger, and Charley Bates.

"What did you bring back with you this morning?" Fagin asked his boys.

"Four silk handkerchiefs," said Bates.

"Ah, I see you've been working hard. Would you like to be able to make such beautiful things, Oliver?"

"Yes, sir, if you'll teach me."

"We'll teach you, don't worry," the others said, laughing.

Oliver didn't see anything funny. He was even more puzzled by the game that his new friends played after breakfast.

Bates Brings Four Silk Handkerchiefs.

Fagin dressed up like an English gentleman and put a wallet, a snuff box, a watch,
and other valuable things in his coat pockets.
Then he picked up a cane and walked around
the room, stopping often as if looking in a
store window. The boys followed behind, careful to keep out of sight. When the "gentleman" stopped, one of the boys stepped on
his foot while another removed all the things
from his pockets. Then they disappeared before the victim could turn around.

"The Dodger and Bates will be great men,"
Fagin told Oliver later. "Take their advice
and do what they do, and you too will be
famous. Now, try to take this handkerchief
out of my back pocket without my feeling it."

Oliver did exactly as he had seen the
Dodger do. Fagin was proud of him and gave
him a shilling. After Oliver had practiced
this trick for several days, he was allowed to
go out with the Dodger and Bates.

A Puzzling Game

Dodger and Bates Steal a Handkerchief.

# CHAPTER 4

# Robbing Mr. Brownlow

"See that old man over there looking at books?" asked the Dodger, leading Oliver to a bookstall on a busy street. "Watch us!"

He and Bates ran toward the gentleman. But the man was so busy reading that he never saw the two boys sneak up behind him and steal his handkerchief from his pocket. While Oliver watched in horror, they ran away. At last he understood what kind of "business" Fagin and his boys engaged in.

Oliver was so upset that he began running as fast as he could. The Dodger and Bates were already out of sight.

"Stop, thief!" yelled the gentleman, thinking that Oliver had stolen his handkerchief.

The people in the streets and even the dogs began to chase him. Someone in the crowd—a young man with purple lips and red sores all over his hands—grabbed Oliver and brought him down upon the pavement. The boy lay there, covered with mud, dust, and blood from a cut lip. A policeman pushed his way through the crowd and roughly pulled Oliver to his feet. He didn't find the handkerchief on the boy's body, but he brought him before a judge anyway.

"I'm afraid the boy is sick, your honor," said Mr. Brownlow, the victim of the robbery. "Don't treat him too badly."

Oliver, indeed, was sick, and he fainted right on the courtroom floor.

Just then, the owner of the bookstall entered the room and swore that Oliver was not the thief.

"The boy is freed!" said the judge.

Chasing a "Thief"

"Call a carriage!" said Mr. Brownlow. "The boy is burning up with fever! I will take him home with me!"

Mr. Brownlow's house was completely different from Fagin's. Everything was new and clean. Oliver slept in a big soft bed, and Mrs. Bedwin, the housekeeper, nursed him back to health in several days.

On the wall of Mr. Brownlow's sitting room hung a picture of a beautiful young woman.

"Look, Mrs. Bedwin!" said Mr. Brownlow. "Oliver looks very much like the person in that picture! The eyes, the head, the mouth—every feature is the same!"

There was, indeed, such a remarkable likeness that Mr. Brownlow could not tear his gaze from Oliver's face.

One evening, Mr. Brownlow called Oliver into his book-lined study.

"I have grown very fond of you, my boy, and I am interested in your future," the gentleman said.

A Remarkable Likeness!

"Then you won't send me away, sir?"

"Of course not, child. But I want to hear all about you—where you were born, where you have been living. . . ."

Just then, Mr. Brownlow's friend arrived. Mr. Grimwig was a stout gentleman with a scowl on his face and a limp in one leg.

"Who is that boy?" asked Mr. Grimwig. "Where does he come from?"

"Tomorrow I shall have a long talk with him and find out," Mr. Brownlow promised. "But now I have an errand for him. I want him to return some books for me to the bookstall. The owner sent too many, and I have to pay for those I'm keeping."

Mr. Brownlow gave Oliver a five-pound note and asked him to bring back the change.

"He won't return," warned Mr. Grimwig. "Mark my words. He'll run off with the books, sell them, and keep the money!"

"Nonsense!" snapped Mr. Brownlow. "Oliver's a good boy."

An Errand for Oliver

"Oliver Will Blab to the Police."

# CHAPTER 5

# Kidnapped!

"Where is Oliver?" roared Fagin when the Dodger and Bates returned from the robbery.

Before they could reply, a very loud voice was heard. It was Bill Sikes, one of Fagin's gang men. Beer stains covered his face and his dirty clothes. His shaggy white dog was at his feet.

When Sikes heard about Oliver and the robbery, he cursed at Fagin for letting the boy go along before he was well trained.

"Oliver will blab to the police and get us all into trouble!" Sikes complained.

The boy had to be found and brought back,

but no member of Fagin's gang wanted to go near the police station. At last they picked on a young woman, Nancy, who often did the gang's dirty work. They ordered her to dress neatly like a woman going to market.

"Where is my little brother?" cried Nancy when she reached the police station.

"There are no little boys here, ma'am," answered an officer.

"Where is he then?" she asked, and she began describing what Oliver looked like.

"Oh, he was driven to the home of a gentleman in Pentonville," said the officer.

When Fagin heard this news, he exploded. "The boy must be found," he cried, "even if we have to kidnap him. None of us will be safe until he is brought back here!"

Bill Sikes and Nancy met Fagin in a tavern. Fagin whispered some instructions to them and gave them some coins. Then they left. They followed Oliver from Mr. Brownlow's house, and just as the boy was

"Where Is My Little Brother?"

passing the bookstall, they ran up to him.

"Oh, my dear brother, I've found you at last!" screamed Nancy, throwing her arms around Oliver's neck. "I've been so worried about you! Why did you run away?"

A crowd gathered to watch them.

"He ran away from his parents, who took such good care of him," Nancy told the people. "He joined a band of robbers and almost broke his dear mother's heart!"

"You naughty child!" scolded one woman.

"Go home now and stay out of trouble!" said another.

"I have no parents," Oliver protested. "I am an orphan."

Suddenly Sikes appeared with his dog. "What's going on here?" he shouted. "Go right home, Oliver. Your mother is waiting!"

"Help! Help!" cried the boy to the crowd. "I don't know these people! Please don't let them take me away!"

"Where did you get these books?"

"Please Don't Let Them Take Me Away!"

demanded Sikes. "I bet you stole them, you rascal!" He grabbed the books from Oliver.

The boy, still weak from his recent illness, was dragged away into the night.

Minutes later, Fagin was emptying Oliver's pockets. "Just look at Oliver's pretty new clothes and his books!" he said. "And what's this? A five-pound note!"

"That money is mine!" growled Sikes.

"No, it's mine!" said Fagin. "You take the books and sell them!"

"If Nancy and I don't get the money, we'll take the boy away again," warned Sikes.

Fagin handed over the money, and Sikes tied the bill in his handkerchief and put it away.

"Don't take the books!" cried Oliver. "They belong to the kind gentleman who took care of me when I had the fever. Keep me here forever if you have to, but return the money and the books, or the gentleman will think I stole them!"

Emptying Oliver's Pockets

"Shut up, Oliver, or I'll set the dog on you!" said Sikes angrily.

"You won't set that dog against the child!" screeched Nancy, as she ran to put her arms around Oliver. "You'll have to kill me first!"

Fagin turned to Oliver, an evil smile on his face. "So you tried to get away from us? Tried to get us into trouble? We'll make sure you don't call the police again!" With that, Fagin struck Oliver on the shoulders with a club and was about to hit him again when Nancy moved between them.

"You've got the boy back. Now leave him alone!" she cried. "You made him a thief. Isn't that enough? I stole things for you when I was even younger than Oliver. Now I'm stuck here forever! What more do you want? Leave the boy alone!"

"That's enough, Nancy!" shouted Fagin. Then turning to Bates, he ordered, "Now, Charley, take Oliver to bed. And be sure he doesn't wear those fancy new clothes again."

Fagin Strikes Oliver with a Club.

FIVE GUINEAS REWARD

A Reward Interests Mr. Bumble.

# CHAPTER 6

# Mr. Bumble Brings Bad News

Mr. Bumble had taken some time off from his position at the workhouse to go to London to take care of a legal problem. At a tavern along the road, he read the following newspaper advertisement:

"FIVE GUINEAS REWARD TO ANYONE WITH INFORMATION LEADING TO A YOUNG BOY, OLIVER TWIST, WHO EITHER RAN AWAY OR WAS KIDNAPPED FROM HIS HOME LAST WEEK. THE MONEY WILL GO TO ANY PERSON WHO FINDS OLIVER OR WHO SHEDS ANY LIGHT ON HIS PAST."

Oliver's description and Mr. Brownlow's address were printed in the paper. Mr. Bumble went directly to the gentleman's home and found Mr. Brownlow and Mr. Grimwig in the study drinking tea.

Mr. Bumble reported to them all that he knew of Oliver's background: the boy had been born of low parentage, he had been an evil and ungrateful child, and he had attacked another boy and then run away in the middle of the night. Mr. Bumble then presented legal papers proving he knew Oliver.

"Thank you for coming," said Mr. Brownlow sadly. "Here are the five guineas. I only wish your report on Oliver had been more favorable."

"He was such a dear, kind, gentle child," said Mrs. Bedwin.

"Think what you will!" Mr. Brownlow told her. "I am so disappointed in that boy that you are never to mention Oliver's name in this house again."

Mr. Brownlow was so hurt that Mr. Grimwig decided not to say, "I told you so."

Disappointing News for Mr. Brownlow

"Don't Try to Run Away Again!"

# CHAPTER 7

# The Housebreaking

"Don't try to run away again!" Fagin warned Oliver the following day. "Just remember, you would have died of hunger if the Dodger hadn't found you along the road! If you get into trouble with the police again, I won't be able to keep you out of jail!"

One night shortly after Oliver's return, Fagin went to visit Sikes and Nancy.

"When can we do the robbery at Chertsey?" asked Fagin.

"It can't be done," said Sikes. "None of the lady's servants will go along with us."

"If we can't do it from the inside, how

about from outside?" asked Fagin, who had his heart set on the job. "I'll give you something extra."

"Okay, it's a deal," replied Sikes. "But I've checked out the house, and I'll need a person small enough to climb through a little window."

"Oliver's just the boy for you!" said Fagin, grinning at Nancy. "I have him well trained by now. He won't cause any more trouble!"

"We'll do it the night after tomorrow then," said Sikes. "There won't be a moon then. Nancy, you bring Oliver to me."

Oliver was reading when Nancy arrived. She sank into a chair and moaned loudly. "God forgive me!" she cried. "This wasn't my idea, but Bill Sikes wants you. Do whatever he tells you to do and keep your mouth shut! He's a mean man and will kill you to save himself!"

"What does he want me for?" asked Oliver.

"For no good," replied the girl.

Nancy Comes to Fetch Oliver.

Nancy grabbed Oliver's hand and led him into the street. He thought of screaming for help or running away. The girl guessed what he was thinking.

"I have tried to help you, but I couldn't," she said, "and you can't help yourself, either. If you want to get away from here, now is not the time. I promised Fagin and Sikes that you would be quiet and would obey them. If you don't listen to them, harm will come to both you and me. I might even be killed! Please don't make me suffer anymore!"

When they came to Sikes's house, the robber held up a pistol. He loaded it and warned Oliver that if he made any noise or tried to run away, he would be shot.

It was 5:00 in the morning when Sikes and Oliver left the house. The boy was given a cape to cover himself with and a big handkerchief to tie around his neck. Sikes patted the pistol in his coat pocket. Oliver turned to take a last look at Nancy, but she sat staring

Taking Oliver to Sikes

at the fireplace.

Sikes and Oliver walked for a whole day until they reached a dark, decaying house at the edge of a river. Inside, they found Toby Crackit, a gang member, resting on an old dirty couch and smoking a long clay pipe.

"Good to see ya, Bill!" said Toby. "Who's the boy?"

"This is Oliver Twist, one of Fagin's boys."

Toby looked at Oliver and smiled at Fagin's choice of a new boy. His dirty fingers, covered with large, cheap rings, twisted the long reddish curls that made a circle around the outside of his bald head.

Sikes bent down and whispered something to Toby. Then the two men tucked pistols into their belts and led Oliver outside into the dark, foggy night.

Oliver walked between the two men until they reached a house surrounded by a wall. Toby climbed up. Then Sikes handed Oliver up to him and followed, himself. Suddenly,

Oliver Meets Toby Crackit.

the boy understood that they were planning a housebreaking and a robbery—maybe even a murder!

"Oh! For God's sake, let me go!" cried Oliver. "Let me run away and die in the fields. I will never tell the police on you! Never! Have mercy on me and don't make me steal!"

Sikes cursed and aimed his pistol at the boy. Toby struck the gun from his hand and dragged Oliver to the house. Sikes forced open the shutter to reveal a window behind it. The window was just big enough for Oliver to squeeze through.

"Take this lantern," said Sikes, handing the light to Oliver. "When you get into the house, go to the front door and open it for us. I'll be holding the gun at your back, so don't try any funny business!"

Oliver crept through the window and jumped down into the room. He made his way to the door to let Toby and Sikes in. As they

A Housebreaking

walked slowly down the hall, Oliver made a decision. He would run upstairs and alert the sleeping family even if it meant his death. Suddenly, from behind him Sikes was shouting.

"Come back! Back! Back!" Sikes called.

Frightened by Sikes's voice and by a loud cry from someone upstairs, Oliver dropped his lantern.

The cry was repeated, a light appeared, and Oliver saw two frightened, half-dressed men at the top of the stairs. Suddenly there was a flash and a loud noise. Oliver staggered back. Sikes fired his own pistol at the two men in the house, then dragged Oliver off the floor and through the door. The boy was bleeding badly.

Oliver heard shouts and pistol shots and felt himself being carried over soft, wet ground. A cold, deadly feeling crept over the boy's heart. The noises grew dim. Then he saw and heard no more.

Oliver Is Shot!

Mr. Bumble Visits Mrs. Corney.

# CHAPTER 8

# A Dying Woman's Secret

It was a snowy, bitter cold night, and Mrs. Corney, who now ran the workhouse where Oliver was born, sat with Mr. Bumble before a cheerful fire, drinking tea.

"It's hard weather, Mrs. Corney, and all the people in the parish complain about not havin' enough food and coals. People are selfish. Here we are, takin' care of these paupers, and they're always askin' for more."

Mrs. Corney enjoyed these visits from Mr. Bumble, he being a single man and she being a widow for 25 years.

Mr. Bumble finished his tea, wiped his

mouth, and suddenly jumped up and kissed the lady on the lips.

"Stop, Mr. Bumble, or I shall scream!" she cried.

But before she had a chance to scream, a knock came at the door and an ugly old woman put her head in.

"If you please, Mrs. Corney," she said, "Old Sally is going fast. She says she has something important to tell you before she dies."

Mrs. Corney was annoyed at being disturbed with her gentleman visitor, but she excused himself and hurried off.

Old Sally lay in a bare attic room, with a dim light burning near the bed. She was twisted with age and trembling with pain.

"Doubt whether she'll last two more hours," said the two attendants, who were stirring the coals in the fireplace.

"Listen, you old hags," snapped Mrs. Corney, "I can't waste my time waiting for all the sick people in this place to die!"

Old Sally Is Dying.

She turned to leave the room when the figure on the bed pulled herself upright and stretched out her arms.

"Don't go!" came a weak voice. "Come over here and let me whisper in your ear. I *must* tell you something before I die."

Mrs. Corney pushed the other old women out the door and went to the bedside.

"Now, listen!" began the dying woman. "In this very room, I once nursed a pretty young thing who was brought in with her feet cut and bleeding and her clothing covered with dirt. She gave birth to a baby boy and then died. The year was, I think. . . ."

"Never mind the year," said Mrs. Corney impatiently. "What about the young woman?"

The woman on the deathbed moaned, and her eyes darted wildly around.

"I remember now!" she cried fiercely. "I robbed that young woman! Before her body was cold, I stole it!"

"Stole what, for God's sake?"

A Dying Woman's Confession

"I stole the only thing the poor creature had. She could have spent it for food or clothes, but she saved it and kept it safe. And it was pure gold!"

"Gold?" Now Mrs. Corney shared Old Sally's excitement. "Go on! Who was the mother? What was it she saved?"

"She asked me to keep it safe for her. She trusted me! But she is dead, and the child may be dead too. If he is, it's my fault. The gold could have saved his life! He would have been treated better if they had known. . . ."

"Known what?" asked Mrs. Corney, who was really puzzled now. "Speak! Speak!"

"The baby boy looked so much like his mother that I could never forget it whenever I saw his face. Poor girl! She was so young!"

The dying woman was out of breath and fell back against her pillow.

"Speak!" shouted Mrs. Corney. "Speak now or it may be too late!"

Old Sally struggled to speak. Her voice was

"Speak! Speak!"

very faint.

"The mother whispered to me that if her baby lived, the day might come when he would not feel so ashamed to have his mother's name mentioned. I pray to Heaven that someone has befriended that poor child! He was so alone!"

"What was the boy's name?" asked Mrs. Corney, who was already beside herself with frustration.

"They *called* him Oliver. And the gold I stole—I took to a pawn. . . ." The old woman's voice trailed off. She grabbed the sheet with both hands, muttered some strange sounds in her throat, and fell back lifeless upon the bed.

"Stone dead, and nothing to tell after all," muttered Mrs. Corney, as she took a small piece of paper out of the dead woman's hands and walked away in disgust, calling the attendants to come in and take care of the body.

What Does the Piece of Paper Mean?

Toby Crackit Returns. . . *Alone*.

# CHAPTER 9

# A Plot Between Fagin and Monks

Fagin, Charley Bates, and the Artful Dodger waited eagerly for news of the robbery.

Toby Crackit dragged himself into the room. He was unshaven, and his clothes and hair were a mess. He dropped slowly into a chair and was silent for several moments.

"How's Bill Sikes?" he said at last.

"What?" screamed Fagin.

"Do you mean to say. . . ." began Toby, turning very pale.

"What's going on, Toby?" cried Fagin. "Where *are* Sikes and the boy? Why haven't they come here?"

"The robbery failed," said Toby quietly. "They fired and hit the boy. We ran away with him. Everyone in the countryside woke up and started to chase us!"

"What happened to the boy?"

"Bill carried him on his back. Then we tried to drag him along between us, but he was too heavy. They were chasing us and were almost upon us. So it became each man for himself. We left Oliver lying in a ditch."

Fagin let out a groan and dashed toward The Three Cripples, the tavern where Sikes usually hung out.

"Have you seen Sikes?" he asked the landlord.

"No, Mr. Fagin."

"Will Monks be here?" asked Fagin. "I must tell him that I have been out taking care of that business matter for him."

"He should be here in ten minutes," said the landlord.

Leaving Oliver in a Ditch

"I can't wait," snapped Fagin. "Tell him he must come to see me tomorrow!"

Fagin went directly to Sikes's house and broke the news to Nancy.

"Oliver's probably better off dead than he is among us," said the girl sadly.

"Listen, Nancy!" cried Fagin in rage. "If Sikes comes back without the boy—if he gets free and doesn't bring Oliver back to me—you have my permission to murder him as soon as he sets foot in this house!"

"Don't bother me, Fagin! Bill has done lots of good jobs for you. If the robbery didn't work this time, it will next time. As for Oliver, I hope he's dead and out of harm's way. As long as Bill and Toby come through all right, the boy is better off lying dead in that ditch."

A dark, shadowy figure stood in Fagin's doorway when he arrived home.

"I've been waiting two hours for you," the man told Fagin impatiently. "Where the devil

Raging About Sikes

have you been?"

"Out on your business all night, Monks," replied Fagin nervously. "But let us talk of this inside where we will not be overheard."

Once inside, Fagin whispered to Monks the details of the unsuccessful robbery.

"The robbery wasn't planned well," said Monks. "Why didn't you keep Oliver here and make a pickpocket of him right away? Or arrange for him to be arrested and sent to prison for life? That would have served my purposes for Oliver Twist."

"But not my purposes, Monks. My interests must be considered too," Fagin complained. "It wasn't easy to train him in the business. He wasn't like the other boys I've taught. I had no hold on him and nothing to frighten him with. What could I do? I sent him out with the Dodger and Charley Bates to pickpocket at the bookstalls, but that failed, and Oliver was caught by the police. But then he was taken into the care of the very man my boys

Different Purposes for Oliver

were robbing."

"*That* was not my fault," snapped Monks.

"I know that," said Fagin. "In fact, if that hadn't happened, you wouldn't have seen Oliver and discovered that he was the boy you were looking for when you knocked him down for the police to nab him. I got him back for you through Nancy, but now she has begun to favor him."

"Thrash Nancy, then!" said Monks, biting down angrily on his swollen purple lips.

"I can't do that, but I'll make Oliver into a thief if he's still alive."

"If he's dead," said Monks, "just remember that I had nothing to do with it! I told you from the start that I don't want any murders. I'd always feel guilty that. . . ."

Suddenly, Monks stopped and stared out the window. "Who's that?" he said. "I saw the shadow of a woman pass outside."

The two men went quickly outside, but no one was in sight.

Has Someone Overheard Them?

Admiring Mrs. Corney's Valuables

# CHAPTER 10

# A Marriage Proposal

While Mr. Bumble waited for Mrs. Corney's return from Old Sally's deathbed, he admired the furniture and many valuables of silver in the room and examined the closets and her drawers. A padlocked box lay in the top drawer. He shook it and heard the clinking of many coins. "I'll do it!" he said firmly.

"I'm so disgusted!" said the lady, appearing at last. "Those old hags are such a nuisance!"

"Relax, Mrs. Corney, and have some wine."

After Mr. Bumble poured it and Mrs. Corney drank half a teacup, Mr. Bumble reached for her hand.

"The master of this workhouse is deathly ill," said Mr. Bumble. "When he dies, someone will have to replace him. I could do the job very well! We could live here together! Will you say the word, dear Mrs. Corney?"

"Ye-ye-yes!"

"Now, let me be of service to you and arrange with Mr. Sowerberry to get a coffin for Old Sally."

The undertaker and his wife were out for the evening when Mr. Bumble arrived. Charlotte, the servant, was serving dinner to Mr. Sowerberry's helper, Noah Claypole. But Noah, who had been drinking while Mr. Sowerberry was out, was not interested in food.

"Come here, Charlotte, and let me kiss you," said Noah.

"What!" cried Mr. Bumble, bursting into the room. "How dare you talk about such things! Leave the room, Charlotte. And you, Noah, tell Mr. Sowerberry to bring a coffin for an old woman tomorrow. Kissing! Indeed!"

"Kissing, Indeed!"

Oliver Goes for Help.

# CHAPTER 11

# Oliver Is Rescued

After the unsuccessful housebreaking, Oliver, wounded and unconscious from a gunshot, was left in a ditch by Toby and Sikes as they made their escape. He awoke hours later with a cry of pain. A bloody bandage was wrapped around his left arm. He struggled to his feet and dragged himself toward the nearest house. It was, in fact, the house they had tried to rob. Oliver staggered across the lawn and knocked faintly at the front door. Giles and Brittles, the servants, jumped at the sound of the knock.

"It's a boy!" exclaimed Giles. "And he's

badly hurt. In fact, he's one of the robbers! I shot him! Let's make sure he doesn't die. I want to see him hanged for his crime!"

"Hush, Giles!" said the lady of the house as she came to the door. "Go into town and fetch a doctor at once!"

There were, in fact, two ladies in the house. One, a stately older woman, was Mrs. Maylie. The other, Rose Maylie, a beautiful girl of about 17, was her niece. The two women followed Doctor Losberne into the room where Oliver lay. They were aghast at how young he was! Rose Maylie bent over the boy and gently pushed his hair from his face.

"How shocking!" said her aunt. "To think that this poor boy was the pupil of robbers and housebreakers!"

"He is so young and fair!" added Rose. "Maybe he has never known a mother's love. Maybe he has never had a home and family. Maybe he was forced into a life of crime because he was starving. We must think

Rose Takes Pity on Oliver.

about this before we send him to jail!"

Oliver was very ill and weak from the loss of blood. But after several days of care by Rose, Mrs. Maylie, and Dr. Losberne, he gradually improved. When some of his strength returned, he told the Maylies about his past. Rose wept bitterly.

"We must do something to help the boy," Rose begged her aunt.

"Yes, we must," said Mrs. Maylie. Then, turning to Dr. Losberne, she asked, "Can you do something?"

"Perhaps if we can convince the servants that they were mistaken when they identified the boy, we can save him when the police come."

The kind-hearted doctor sent for the two servants.

"Giles and Brittles," said Dr. Losberne, "can you swear that the boy with the robbers was Oliver? Could you really identify him in the darkness with all the gunfire?"

Oliver Tells About His Past.

The servants admitted that they couldn't be absolutely certain. So when policemen arrived at the house to investigate the housebreaking, no one could identify the boy. So no charges were pressed against Oliver. After all, it was difficult not to pity the poor little boy. He looked so helpless and innocent lying there in bed! Could he really have wanted to rob the house?

Oliver recovered quickly from his wounds and entered upon the happiest period of his life since his stay with Mr. Brownlow. The Maylies treated him like a member of their own family. And when spring came, they took him to their cottage in the country.

One day Dr. Losberne took the boy to Mr. Brownlow's house. Oliver wanted very much to explain why he hadn't returned with the change from the books. Alas! The house was empty, and a "For Rent" sign hung on the front door.

"Where has Mr. Brownlow gone?" the

Looking for Mr. Brownlow

doctor asked a neighbor.

"He packed his things and left for the West Indies just six weeks ago, sir. His house-keeper, Mrs. Bedwin, and his friend, Mr. Grimwig, went with him."

Oliver was disappointed, but he kept busy, helping Rose and her aunt with their house-hold chores. He also learned to read and write. He spent many happy hours running along the country roads, picking flowers, and feeding the birds. In the evenings, he listened to Rose play the piano.

The happy days ended suddenly when Rose developed a terrible fever. Her hands were too weak to play the piano, and her face was deathly pale. Each day she got weaker.

Finally, Mrs. Maylie sent Oliver running to the inn in town four miles away to leave a letter with the postman for Dr. Losberne. As Oliver stood outside the inn watching the mail rider saddle his horse, a horrible-looking man with purple lips and red sores on his hands

Rose Develops a Terrible Fever.

came running towards him from the inn.

"Curses on your head!" cried the man wildly. "Death on your heart, you imp! Why can't I be free of you!"

When the man came at Oliver with his fists raised, Oliver turned on his heels and raced away. He turned his head back long enough to see the man fall to the ground, writhing and foaming in a fit.

Rose's fever became dangerously high. When Dr. Losberne arrived, he offered very little hope for her recovery. "There is nothing to do but pray," he said sadly.

Rose fell into a deep sleep. The doctor stayed by her bedside for three days and three nights. On the fourth day, he left the room and came out to Mrs. Maylie.

"The worst is over," he cried happily. "The fever has broken. God has blessed Rose. She will live!"

Oliver was overcome with joy. He went out to gather the most beautiful flowers he could

A Horrible-Looking Man Comes at Oliver.

find for Rose's sickroom. When he returned to the cottage, he saw a handsome young man climb down from a coach. It was Mrs. Maylie's son, Harry.

The young man rushed to Mrs. Maylie and cried, "Mother, why didn't you write to me sooner? What if Rose had died?"

"You know why I waited, Harry. If a rich and successful man marries a lady upon whose name there is a stain because the story of her birth is doubtful, he will be sorry later in life. I love you, my son, and I love Rose too. . .dearly. But evil people will not let you forget her past, even though it is not her fault. And Rose, too, will suffer because you will turn against her."

"I would never turn against Rose!" cried Harry angrily. "She is my life and my happiness! Let her decide if she wants me, Mother!"

Mrs. Maylie agreed that Harry would be permitted to see Rose as soon as she was well

Harry Maylie Arrives.

enough to leave her room.

The following evening as Oliver sat on the front porch, half-awake, half-dozing, Fagin's face flashed in front of him.

"Come away, my boy," came the voice of Fagin.

Then another man appeared with Fagin— the horrible-looking man who had tried to attack Oliver outside the inn.

In an instant the two men were gone, and Oliver leaped into the garden, screaming for help.

Harry Maylie knew Oliver's history and understood his fright. He and Giles combed the hedges, the ditches, and the footpaths, but there was not even a trace of footsteps.

"It must have been a dream, Oliver," said Harry when they returned.

"No, it was really Fagin," the boy insisted. "Fagin and the man who cursed at me when I went to post the letter to Dr. Losberne!"

The search continued, but in vain.

Faces Flash in Front of Oliver.

"I Couldn't Bear to Have You Die."

# CHAPTER 12

# A Love Story

When Rose fully recovered from her fever, Harry Maylie had a long talk with her.

"I wish you hadn't come," she said softly, with tears welling up in her eyes.

"I know, my dear, but I was so worried when I heard about your illness. I couldn't bear to have you die and not hear how much I love you."

"It is just that I want you to devote yourself to more noble things, dear Harry, for your future is so bright!"

"My greatest desire for my future is to win your heart, my dear Rose! I have loved you since we were just children."

"You must remember me only as your childhood friend, but you must forget me as the object of your love, Harry."

"Why have you made this decision, Rose?"

"I must protect you from the evil that would befall you if people learned the circumstances of my birth."

"But do you *love* me, Rose?"

"Yes, I do, but we shouldn't meet again. You are destined for much success in public life. I cannot mix with people who would scorn me because of my background. No, you must go!"

"I shall go. But I ask only one promise. Within a year let me talk to you once more about this matter."

"Then let it be so, but you will not change my mind."

Harry took Rose in his arms and kissed her tenderly on the lips. Then he rushed from the room.

A Tender Good-Bye Kiss

Mr. Bumble Meets a Stranger.

# CHAPTER 13

# A Chance Meeting

Mr. Bumble and Mrs. Corney were married. He was promoted to the job of master of the workhouse, and he became sterner than ever.

One night, after a violent quarrel with his new wife, Mr. Bumble went to a tavern for a drink. The only customer there, a tall, dark man with an ugly face and sharp eyes, stared at him. His hands, all covered with red sores, played nervously with his glass.

"Were you looking for me when you peered through the window just now?" asked the stranger.

"No," answered Mr. Bumble, "unless you are. . . ." By stopping, Mr. Bumble hoped the man would reveal his name.

"I guess you weren't, or you would have known my name," said the stranger. "Well, don't ask for it! I recognize you, though. Aren't you a parish official here?"

"Yes, I'm master of the workhouse," said Mr. Bumble proudly.

"Oh! What luck! I came here today to find you, and by some stroke of luck you wandered into this very room. I need some information from you. I'll pay for it."

The stranger pushed some coins across the table, and Mr. Bumble pocketed them.

The stranger continued, "Think back on a scene in the workhouse one night about 12 years ago. A woman gave birth to a baby boy and then died. The baby was left for the parish to take care of."

"There were many such cases," said Mr. Bumble.

The Stranger Pays for Information.

"This one grew into a weak, pale-faced boy who was sent to work for a coffin-maker and later ran away to London. . . ."

"Oh, you must mean Oliver! Oliver Twist!"

"Now tell me where I can find the hag who took care of his mother."

"She died last winter."

The stranger gazed into space and bit down hard on his swollen purple lips that already had teeth marks in them. Mr. Bumble couldn't decide whether he was disappointed or relieved. Suddenly, the stranger rose to leave. Mr. Bumble was cunning. He sensed that he could make some more money off the man.

"Wait, my friend," said Mr. Bumble. "Perhaps I know something more." Mr. Bumble remembered the day Old Sally died. It was the very day he had proposed marriage to Mrs. Corney. He wasn't sure what the dying woman had told his wife, but he knew it had something to do with Oliver's mother.

"Perhaps I Know Something More."

Then, when he saw the stranger's interest, he continued, "Another woman shared the old hag's secrets before she died. Perhaps she can give you more information."

"Where can I find this woman?" asked the stranger eagerly.

"Only through me. I'll bring her to you."

"Here's the address. Come at 9:00 tomorrow evening."

Mr. Bumble looked at the paper. "There's no name. What name do I ask for?"

"Monks!" replied the stranger as he hurried away.

An Address with No Name

The Meeting Place

# CHAPTER 14

# An Important Piece of Evidence

It was a humid, cloudy evening when Mr. and Mrs. Bumble turned off the main road and walked toward a shabby, decaying house built on a swamp near the river. They wore long dark cloaks to hide themselves from view. Just as they reached the house, a thunder storm struck and lightning flashed across the sky.

"Halloa there!" called Monks, coming out a door on the second story.

Within minutes, Monks appeared at a small door on the main level and led them inside. They followed him up a ladder into a small room with a shuttered window and a table with three chairs.

"Let's get right down to business," said Monks, staring at Mrs. Bumble. "What did the old hag tell you the night she died?"

"What is the information worth to you?" asked Mrs. Bumble calmly.

"That depends on what you tell me."

"Before I tell you anything, I'll take 25 pounds in gold!" said the lady firmly.

Mr. Bumble was amazed at his wife's daring. In fact, he was somewhat frightened. But Monks hesitated only an instant before turning over the money.

Then Mrs. Bumble began to speak. "Old Sally and I were alone when death came to her. She spoke of a young mother who had given birth to a baby boy in the very bed in which Sally was then lying. The child became known as Oliver Twist."

"Go on!" said Monks with excitement.

"Old Sally robbed the mother as soon as

"Let's Get Right Down to Business."

she died. She stole what the young mother had asked with her final breath that she keep for the sake of the baby."

"What was it?"

"A piece of gold jewelry."

Monks leaned forward. "What did she do with it? Sell it? Where? To whom?"

"As she tried to tell me all this, she fell back and died," said Mrs. Bumble.

"Without saying more?" cried Monks in a rage. "That's a lie!"

"She didn't say another word," said Mrs. Bumble, unafraid of the stranger's violence. "That's the honest truth. But she did grab my gown with a hand that was clutching a scrap of paper."

"What did it say?"

"Nothing. It was a pawnbroker's ticket," explained the woman. "Whatever she had owned, she must have pawned to get money."

"What did you do then?"

"The ticket was due to be paid in two days,

"That's a Lie!"

so I went to the pawnbroker and paid the loan plus the interest to recover the jewelry."

"Where is it now?" cried Monks excitedly.

"Right here!" said Mrs. Bumble, producing a small box. It contained a plain gold wedding ring and a little gold locket, in which were two locks of hair.

"The locket has the name 'Agnes' carved on it," added Mrs. Bumble. "There's a space left for the last name. Then comes the date, which is within a year before the child was born."

Monks seemed satisfied, and Mr. Bumble sighed in relief that he would not have to return the 25 pounds if Monks were not satisfied with the information. Suddenly Monks jumped up and threw the table aside. He opened a trap door in the wooden floor and showed his visitors the swiftly flowing river below their feet. Monks placed the box and a heavy rock inside a handkerchief, tied it up, and dropped it into the water. He watched as

Monks Drops the Evidence into the Water.

the rock pulled it to the bottom of the river.

When the box disappeared from sight, Monks closed the trap door and glared at the Bumbles. "Just remember, this secret is between the three of us," he warned. "If you tell it to anyone else, your life will be worth nothing! Now get away from here as fast as you can!"

Mr. and Mrs. Bumble were happy to go.

"Get Away from Here as Fast as You Can!"

Sikes Accuses Fagin of Plotting.

# CHAPTER 15

# Nancy Warns Rose Maylie

It was the night after Monks had met the Bumbles. Bill Sikes, tired and ill, lay on a filthy bed in a tiny, barely-furnished room. He wore a dirty dressing gown and had a stiff, black beard a week old. His mood was ugly because of illness and because a streak of bad luck had brought about this poverty.

Fagin had just stopped in to see Bill and Nancy.

"Where've you been all week, Fagin?" asked Bill. "You were plotting while I was lying here helplessly."

"I was away from London on business,"

said Fagin. "I wouldn't forget you."

"Well, I need some money. If it hadn't been for Nancy, I would have died."

"I'll send some money around with the Artful Dodger," said Fagin.

"No, you won't. He might just forget to come or find some excuse to spend it. No, I'll send Nancy home with you to fetch it."

While the girl was at Fagin's house waiting for him to count out some money for Bill, Monks arrived. The two men climbed upstairs to another room, but Nancy followed and listened in at the door.

By the time the two men came down, she was putting on her shawl and bonnet, preparing to leave. She dared not look at Fagin as he dropped the coins into her hand. She was too frightened at what she had heard upstairs.

Nancy was weak and pale by the time she reached Sikes's room with the money. She tried to hide her upset from Sikes, who was

Nancy Listens at the Door.

only interested in the money, but the house-breaker began to question her.

"You look pale as a corpse. What's the matter?"

"Nothing," she replied and tried to force gaiety into her voice.

Later that night, Nancy dropped some sleeping powder into Sikes's drink. As soon as he dozed off, she put on her bonnet and shawl and left the house.

"I pray I'm not too late," she murmured as she walked into a fancy hotel in the West-End of London.

"I would like to see Miss Maylie," she told the doorman breathlessly. He looked at her outfit and pushed her towards the door.

"Please! I *must* see her!" Nancy cried.

"Whom shall I say is calling?"

"It's no use giving a name."

"And what business are you on?"

"It's no use mentioning that, either." Nancy looked around desperately at the

Sleeping Powder for Sikes

housemaids who had gathered at the door. "Won't someone here carry a message for a poor girl like me?"

One of the softhearted servants agreed.

"What is the message?" she asked Nancy.

"Tell Miss Maylie that I would like to speak to her alone. It's very important!"

Nancy thought of the great gulf that separated a woman like herself from a refined lady like Rose Maylie. Nancy had spent all her life in the streets and sinful places around London, but she still had some pride.

"It's not easy to get in to see you," she told Rose. "If I'd become angry at the way I was treated and gone away, you would have been sorry later on."

"I'm sorry if someone treated you harshly," Rose replied. "Now please tell me why you wish to see me." Her sweet face and gentle voice surprised Nancy, and the girl burst into tears.

"I am about to put my life and the lives of

Nancy Tries to Get to See Rose Maylie.

others in your hands," Nancy sobbed. "I am the girl who dragged little Oliver back to Fagin's place on the night he left Mr. Brownlow's house in Pentonville."

"You!" exclaimed Rose.

"Yes, and there is more. I have run away from those people who would murder me if they knew I was here, telling you what I overheard. Do you know a man named Monks?"

"No," said Rose.

"He knows you and knew you were here. Only by hearing him mention this place was I able to find you."

"Yes," said Rose, "I understand. Go on."

"Soon after Oliver was put into your house on the night of the robbery, I began suspecting Monks. I listened to a talk between him and Fagin. I learned that Monks had seen Oliver accidentally with two of our boys on the day we first lost him. Monks recognized Oliver as the child that he was watching for,

Nancy Confesses Kidnapping Oliver.

but I don't know why he was watching for him. He made a deal with Fagin, that if Oliver were returned, he would give Fagin a large sum of money. Fagin was to get an even larger sum if he made Oliver into a thief."

"A thief? For what purpose?" asked Rose.

"Monks saw my shadow on the wall as I tried to hear about that, so I had to run away. Then I didn't see Monks again until last night."

"What happened then?"

"He came again to see Fagin. I listened to their conversation from another room. Monks said that the only proof of Oliver's real identity lay at the bottom of the river and that the old hag who received the proof was dead. Then Monks laughed and said he had Oliver's money safely for himself now, but that it would have been fun to make the boy a thief and have him jailed. It seems Monks wanted to get everything from his father's

Monks's Plot Is Revealed.

will and with Oliver out of the way, he could. He said Fagin could arrange for the boy to be jailed and hung after the old thief had made a profit out of him!"

Rose couldn't believe her ears!

"There's more," said Nancy, speaking quickly, for she had to get back before she was missed. "Monks said that he would kill Oliver himself if he could get away with it without getting caught. But since he couldn't, he would always be on the watch for Oliver to make sure he didn't take advantage of his inheritance. Monks even told Fagin, 'I may harm him yet. You can't imagine what traps I shall set for my young brother Oliver.' "

"His brother!" exclaimed Rose.

"Yes! And he said you would probably pay hundreds of thousands of pounds, if you had them, to find out who Oliver really is. And now I must leave!"

"But why do you wish to return to these people who have treated you so horribly? If

"His Brother!"

you'll let me call a gentleman from the next room, he can take you to a safe place."

"Thank you, dear lady, but I must go back. There is one man among the bunch who is even more desperate than the rest. If the others found out that I had told you all this, they would surely kill him. I can't forsake him even to be saved from the dreadful life I lead."

"But what good will this information be when you are gone? How can Oliver be helped?"

"You *must* have some wise friend who will keep your secret and advise you what to do," Nancy replied.

"At least tell me where I can find you if I need to," begged Rose.

"Will you promise that you will come alone and not tell anyone else where you are going and not allow anyone to follow or watch you?"

"I promise," said Rose.

A Gentleman in the Next Room Can Help.

"Very well, then. Every Sunday night, from 11:00 until midnight, I will walk on London Bridge if I am alive."

"Please then, take some money," said Rose, "so you can live as an honest woman."

"Not a penny," said Nancy. "But God bless you, sweet lady."

Nancy hurried off quickly into the night, and Rose sank into a chair to collect her thoughts.

Nancy Refuses Rose's Money.

"I Saw Mr. Brownlow At Last!"

# CHAPTER 16

# Mr. Brownlow Learns the Truth

Rose loved Oliver and wanted to help him regain his good name, but she didn't want to cause Nancy's death by giving away her secret. She remained deep in thought.

"I saw Mr. Brownlow at last!" said Oliver, bursting into the room. "I was out walking with Giles, and I saw Mr. Brownlow get out of a coach and go into a house. I was trembling so, that I could not go up to him, but I wrote down the address! Now I must go there!"

"We'll go right away!" said Rose, realizing that the gentleman might be very helpful on her own business.

She ordered a coach immediately, and when they arrived at the Craven Street address Oliver had written down, Rose told Oliver to wait in the coach while she went inside alone to see Mr. Brownlow.

Rose was shown into the study where she found the kindly-looking Mr. Brownlow with his friend, Mr. Grimwig, who looked as grim as ever.

"My name is Rose Maylie," she began. "You once showed great kindness to a very dear young friend of mine, and I thought you might be interested in hearing how he is. His name is Oliver Twist."

Mr. Brownlow was too surprised to speak for several moments. Finally, he drew his chair closer to Rose.

"My dear lady," he said kindly, "if you have it in your power to change the bad impression that I have of that child, please tell me what you know. I have tried every way

Rose Calls On Mr. Brownlow.

possible to find him."

Rose told him everything that had befallen Oliver since he left Mr. Brownlow's house.

"You bring welcome news, indeed!" said Mr. Brownlow. "But where is the boy now?"

"He's waiting in the coach just outside."

Mr. Brownlow dashed outside and returned with Oliver. Then he sent for Mrs. Bedwin. It was a joyous reunion indeed!

While Oliver was busily chatting with Mrs. Bedwin, Rose told the men about Nancy. Mr. Grimwig wanted to have the girl arrested.

"Calm down," said Mr. Brownlow. "Having all those scoundrels arrested is not our first concern. We must be careful. We must find out who Oliver's parents were and then get his inheritance returned to him. Moving against the girl will do no good. We have to get this fellow Monks alone and make him confess. After all, he is not one of this gang of robbers. But first we must see the girl and ask her to show us who Monks is—or to

A Joyous Reunion

describe him and where he hangs out so we can find him ourselves. We can do this without giving her secret away, without bringing any harm upon her."

They decided to tell Dr. Losberne, Mrs. Maylie, and Harry Maylie about these plans, but to say nothing to Oliver himself.

"I will go to any expense," said Mrs. Maylie, "if it means helping Oliver."

"Good!" exclaimed Mr. Brownlow. "Then I shall go with Rose on Sunday night to meet with this girl Nancy on London Bridge."

Mr. Brownlow Reveals His Plans.

On the Road to London

# New Members for the Gang

On the very night that Nancy visited Rose, Noah Claypole and Charlotte set out on the road to London. They carried on their backs whatever belongings they could manage. After traveling along the main road for a while, they turned off into narrow streets so that no one could follow their trail.

"I'm so tired," complained Charlotte. "When we will get there?"

"Don't whine, Charlotte. If it weren't for me, ya never would have escaped from that place. Ya took the money from Sowerberry's till, didn't ya?"

"I took it for *you*, Noah dear."

"Well, I'm lettin' ya hold it, aren't I?" said Noah.

In fact, Noah had planned for her to hold it, so that if they were caught, she would go to jail and he would go free!

"Here's The Three Cripples," said Noah. "I heard that it's a good tavern."

He took the heavy bundle off Charlotte's back and carried it himself to make a better impression when they walked in. Seated at the bar was an old man who the bartender called Fagin. Noah and Charlotte sat down at a table in a small back room and ordered some beer and cold meat.

"Look, we got visitors from the country," said Barney, the bartender, letting Fagin look through a small opening between the two rooms.

"I'm interested in those people," said Fagin. "Look how the girl obeys the man; he knows how to train 'em. Don't make any noise. I

A Good Tavern

want to hear what they're saying!"

"So I mean to live like a gentleman," Noah was telling Charlotte. "No more coffin-making. And you should live like a lady."

"That sounds fine, Noah, but it's not every day that we can empty tills and get away with it!"

"There's other things besides tills that can be emptied—people's pockets, houses, mail coaches, banks. . . ."

"You can't do all that by yourself, Noah!"

"Well, I mean to get in with some gang that does them sort of things. You'd be helpful too, Charlotte. You're a clever woman."

That was all Fagin needed to hear. He entered the room, bowed to the couple, and sat down at the nearest table. He took a long drink from the mug Barney had set before him and whispered in Noah's direction, "One has to empty a lot of tills to eat and drink like this all the time!"

Noah froze and turned pale.

Fagin Overhears Noah's Plans.

"Don't worry!" added Fagin with a laugh. "I'm the only one that heard ya talkin'. You're lucky that it was only me!"

"Well, *she* took the money, not me."

"Doesn't matter who took it. I'm that way myself, and I've taken a fancy to you and the young woman. All the people at The Cripples are in the same kind of business as I am. You're in a perfectly safe place! In fact, if you want to join us, I can recommend you. We don't usually take country people, but we need some helpers. What part of the business are you interested in?"

"Would I have to hand over our money if we wanted to join?" asked Noah.

"That's the only way," replied Fagin. "You couldn't spend it anyway. The police and the bank probably have the numbers on the bills. We'd have to send them out of the country."

"Well, what are your wages?" Noah asked.

"Live like a gentleman—board and lodging, pipes and spirits free—half of all you earn

"I Heard Ya Talkin'."

and half of all the young woman earns," replied Fagin.

"I'd like to start with something very easy," said Noah. "Not too dangerous."

"How about spying on some people?"

"That's okay, but it wouldn't pay by itself."

"How about the old ladies, then? You can snatch their pocketbooks and parcels and run right around the corner."

"The problem with that is they scream and scratch a good deal. Isn't there something else?"

"I have it!" cried Fagin, slapping Noah's knee. "The children! Their mothers always send them on errands with sixpence and shillings. All you have to do is grab the money from their hands, knock them down, and walk away."

"That sounds perfect," cried Noah. "Now what time shall I come to meet your friends?"

"Tomorrow at ten," said Fagin. "See you then!"

Fagin Has the Perfect Idea!

Only Fagin Is There.

# CHAPTER 18

# The Dodger Is Caught

The next night at ten, when Noah and Charlotte entered the small room behind The Three Cripples bar, only Fagin was there.

"So it was really you, not a friend, who was to meet us," Noah said to Fagin. "I thought as much last night."

"Every man is his own friend," answered Fagin, with a sly smile. "Remember, we're all in this together! If one person squeals, we might all get caught! We're already in enough trouble. And yesterday, the Dodger, one of my best boys, got caught with a silver snuffbox!"

Charley Bates entered the room, his face twisted with sadness. "It's all over for the Dodger," he announced. "The owner of the snuffbox identified him, and he goes on trial today. Too bad he couldn't have gone out in a blaze of glory by stealing something really valuable, instead of with a halfpenny snuffbox. Now his talents are lost to us forever!"

"Here's a golden opportunity for you to help us out," said Fagin to Noah. "Master Bates and I couldn't possibly visit the Dodger at the courthouse. But nobody knows you and, with the proper clothing, no one would suspect your connection with us."

"I don't know. . . ." began Noah.

"What good are you?" asked Bates angrily. "You want to eat well without doin' any work!"

At last Noah agreed to go. Fagin dressed him in velvet pants, leather leggings, a wagoner's coat, and a felt hat. That way, he

Bates Brings Bad News.

would look like a simple country fellow, calling at the courthouse out of curiosity. Bates told him what the Dodger looked like and then led him through a maze of narrow streets to within a block of the courthouse.

Noah walked into a large crowd in the dirty, foul-smelling room at the courthouse. On a raised platform at one end of the room was the prisoner's dock. A box for witnesses was in the middle and a desk for the judge on the right. A clerk was reading out jail sentences for other prisoners in the dock. Finally the Dodger was brought into the dock, blustering all the way.

"What are my rights?" he cried. "I'm an Englishman, after all!"

"Hold your tongue and you'll find out!" snapped the jailer.

"What's the charge?" asked the judge.

"A pickpocket case, your honor."

"Where are the witnesses?"

A policeman and an old gentleman

The Dodger Is Brought into Court.

appeared.

"Have you anything to say, boy?" the judge asked the Dodger.

"I wouldn't even bother to discuss this stupid matter. But my lawyer will have plenty to say. You won't get away with treating me like this!"

"Take him away and lock him up!" the judge ordered the jailer.

The Dodger was dragged off cursing, and Noah returned to make a full report to Fagin and Bates.

"Take Him Away and Lock Him Up!"

"You're Not Going Anywhere!"

# CHAPTER 19

# A Suspect in the Group

All Sunday evening, Nancy sat listening to
Bill Sikes and Fagin discuss their plans. Finally at 11:00, she put on her bonnet and
prepared to go out to meet Rose Maylie.

"Where is she going at this hour?" Fagin
asked Sikes.

"Just to get a breath of fresh air,"
answered Nancy.

"You're not going anywhere!" shouted
Sikes. "Sit down!"

"Let me go!" Nancy screamed. "I just want
some air."

"There's enough air in here," cried Sikes as

he grabbed her arms, dragged her to a chair, and forced her to sit down. Despite her pleas and cries and struggles, Nancy could not get loose. By the time the clock struck midnight, she had given up hope of getting out.

"The girl has really gone crazy!" said Sikes to Fagin. "Why do you think she was so eager to go out?"

"Women are stubborn," said the old man. "She's harder to train than most of them."

Fagin thought about Nancy all the way home—her temper tantrums, her lack of interest in the gang's activities, and her desires to go out alone so often. It almost seemed like she was tired of living with Sikes. The girl, in fact, may have already found a new boyfriend, even though Sikes had kept her alive as a young child and saved her from a life in the workhouse. If she had a new boyfriend, Fagin wanted to find out who he was. And Noah Claypole was the perfect man to spy on her!

Nancy Has No Hope of Getting Out.

A Very Important Job for Noah

# CHAPTER 20

# A Midnight Meeting

"You did an excellent job with the children," Fagin told Noah the following morning. "Six shillings and ninepence halfpenny on the very first day! Now I need you for a very important job."

"I hope it's nothing dangerous. . . ."

"Not in the least. All you have to do is follow a young woman. I want to know where she goes, who she sees, what she. . . ."

"How much is it worth to ya?" Noah asked.

"If you do it well, I'll give you one pound. And that's paying a lot for such an easy job."

"Who is this woman?"

"One of us."

"You don't trust her anymore?"

"She has found some new friends, and I must find out who they are," replied Fagin. "She is at The Three Cripples now. I'll point her out to you."

Once done, Noah followed Nancy all week. But she met no one. Finally on Sunday night, Noah followed Nancy out of The Cripples. She walked swiftly in the direction of London Bridge. Noah followed behind at a safe distance.

The church bells chimed midnight when a young woman and a gray-haired gentleman got out of a carriage and walked toward Nancy.

"Not here," whispered Nancy, as she motioned toward the steps leading down from the bridge. They followed her down.

"Why weren't you here last Sunday night?" asked Mr. Brownlow.

"I couldn't come. Bill Sikes forced me to

Noah Follows Nancy.

stay home. The only way I was able to go see Miss Maylie at her hotel was by putting sleeping powder in his drink."

"Did he awake before you returned?"

"No. Neither he nor any of them suspect me."

"Good! Now, listen. Miss Maylie has told me your secret. I believe you, and I want you to trust me. Have no fear. Our plan is to make this fellow Monks tell us what he knows. But if Monks cannot be found, or if he won't talk, you must deliver Fagin into our hands."

"Fagin? No, I can't do that! I will never do it!"

"Why not?" asked Mr. Brownlow.

"Fagin has led a bad life, but so have I. He has never turned against me, and I have no reason to turn against him."

"In that case," said Mr. Brownlow, "put Monks into my hands and I will deal with him."

Mr. Brownlow Reveals Their Plans.

"But what if Monks turns against the others?" gasped Nancy.

"No matter what he tells us, we will not turn against your friends. We only want to know about Oliver. Now, will you help us find him?"

"Yes," said Nancy with a sigh. "Monks is tall and strong. He has dark hair and eyes. He's only about 28 years old, but his face is old and sunken. He has terrible fits, so his lips are purple and covered with teeth marks. Sometimes, in these fits, he bites his hands too. So they are covered with wounds. He wears a large cloak, but if you look at his throat, you can see a broad red mark like a burn. . . ."

Both Mr. Brownlow and Rose gasped.

"Do you know Monks?" asked Nancy.

"I think we do, but please continue," said Mr. Brownlow.

"Well, he spends a lot of time at a tavern called The Three Cripples. You should be

A Familiar Description!

able to find him there."

"You have given us valuable help," said Mr. Brownlow kindly. "How may we serve you now?"

"You can do nothing to help me," sobbed Nancy. "I am beyond hope."

"Maybe you'll change your mind. We can offer you a safe place to stay, either in England or abroad. We can put you beyond the reach of Fagin and the others. Leave now with us, while there is still time!"

"Thank you for your kindness, sir, but I am chained to my old life and even though I hate it, I cannot leave it. Now I must go before anyone misses me. Good night!"

Once Nancy had left the bridge, and Mr. Brownlow and Rose had climbed into their carriage, Noah Claypole crept slowly from his hiding place. Seeing that the bridge was deserted, he darted down the street towards Fagin's house as fast as his legs would carry him.

Leaving the Bridge

"You Were Followed Tonight."

# CHAPTER 21

# The Murder

As soon as Noah reported back to Fagin, the old man immediately sent for Sikes and told him the whole story about Nancy's midnight meeting on the bridge.

Sikes was enraged as he raced home and into the bedroom where Nancy lay asleep. He grabbed her by the throat and dragged her to the floor.

"What's wrong, Bill? What have I done?" she gasped.

"As if you didn't know! You were followed tonight. Every word was overheard."

"Then spare my life as I spared yours and

Fagin's!" cried the girl, clinging to him. "Listen to me! The gentleman and the lady offered to send me to a good home in a foreign country. Let me ask them to do the same for you. We could leave here forever and start a new life!"

She held on to him so tightly that it was a great effort for Sikes to loosen her grip. He finally freed one of his hands and reached for his pistol. He realized, however, that the shot would attract attention and he'd be caught. So, instead, he brought the pistol down with all his might on Nancy's head.

She staggered and fell, blinded by the blood from the gash in her forehead. With her final breath, she pleaded for mercy. But Sikes covered his eyes with his hand, grabbed a heavy club, and struck her dead!

Sikes sat for hours staring at the body. Finally, when the sun's rays entered the room, he roused himself and slowly got up. He lit a fire, and when it was burning brightly, he

Nancy Pleads for Mercy.

threw the club into it. Then he washed the blood off himself and off his clothes.

He didn't dare stay there any longer. So he locked up the house and set out with his dog. He walked for miles, out of London and into the country, his dog trotting at his side.

By nine o'clock that night he came to a town, where he hoped to stop and rest. He saw a mail coach standing before the little post office. All the people were gathered around it, talking about a murder in London.

This was not a safe town for a murderer to rest in, so Sikes decided to go back to London. Maybe he could get lost in the big city. Maybe he could even wangle some money from Fagin to escape to France. First, however, he had to get rid of the dog, in case any descriptions were out for a man with a dog. He tried to put a rope around the dog's neck to drown him in a pond. But the animal, sensing the plan, ran away across the fields.

And Sikes continued the journey alone.

Where Can a Murderer Go?

"How Dare You Kidnap Me!"

# CHAPTER 22

# Monks Tells His Story

A coach pulled up in front of Mr. Brownlow's house. Mr. Brownlow got out and waited as two strong men dragged Monks from the coach into the house.

"How dare you kidnap me in the street!" cried Monks.

"I had my reasons," said Mr. Brownlow. "I gave you the choice of coming here or surrendering to the police. You agreed to come quietly with us. If you try to leave here now, I'll have you arrested!"

"What kind of treatment is this from my father's oldest friend?" asked Monks.

"It is *because* I am your father's oldest friend that I am treating you rather gently now, Edward Leeford—though you should be ashamed to bear that name. Your father's sister would have been my wife, if she had lived. I have forgotten neither him nor her."

"But what do you want with me?" asked Monks.

"You have a brother," said Mr. Brownlow, "a brother whose name I whispered to you in the street."

"I have no brother," replied Monks. "I am an only child. Surely you know that."

"What I *do* know is that your father, as a young man, was forced by his family's ambition into a wretched, unhappy marriage with a woman a good deal older than he. You were born from that miserable marriage. Later, your parents separated. Then, about 15 years ago, when your father was only 31 and you were about 11, your father made a new friend—an older gentleman—whose wife had

"You Have a Brother."

recently died and left him with two daughters. One was a beautiful girl of 19 and the other, only 2 or 3 years old. Your father fell in love with the elder daughter."

Monks was getting more and more nervous, but Mr. Brownlow continued. "And that daughter fell deeply in love with him. Then one of your rich relatives died and left your father a large sum of money. He had to go to Rome to settle this relative's business. Your mother was living a frivolous life in Paris at the time, but when she heard about all that money, she followed your father to Rome, bringing you with her. Your father died suddenly the day after she arrived, leaving no will—*no will*—so all his money and property went to your mother and you."

Monks leaned forward in his chair and held his breath.

"But before your father left for Rome, he came to see me," continued Mr. Brownlow.

"I never heard of that!" said Monks.

Monks's Father Fell in Love.

"He left with me some of his possessions which he could not take along on his hasty trip to Rome. Among those possessions was a portrait of the young woman he loved—a portrait that he, himself, had painted. His one wish was to sell off everything he owned, give all his wealth to you and your mother, then start a new life elsewhere with the woman he loved. He said he would write and tell me more, but I never heard from him again.

"A short while after his death, I tried to locate this young woman for she was carrying his child. I wanted to give them both a home with me. But when I got to her father's home, I learned that the family had left London the week before."

Monks breathed easier, but only for a moment.

"When that child—a boy—was born in a workhouse, his mother died, alone and friendless. He was a sickly child as he grew. Yet

A Portrait of the Woman He Loved

some strange fate brought him to me, and I was able to save him from a life of evil."

"What?" cried Monks.

"When he was in my house recovering from a fever, I was shocked by the likeness between him and the portrait I just told you about. Your evil friends, however, kidnapped him back before I could learn his history. . . ."

"B-but you don't have proof that a child was born to my father and this girl," stammered Monks.

"I do have proof about that," explained Mr. Brownlow. "Your father *did* have a will, even though everyone thought not. But your mother destroyed it before her death, but not before she told you her secret. The will said something about a child likely to be born. You, in fact, later saw the child and recognized him because he looked so much like your father. You then went to the place of his birth and managed to get your hands on the proof his identity. Then you threw that proof

"B-but You Don't Have Proof. . . ."

into the river. You are an unworthy son, a coward and a liar—a man who mixes with thieves and murderers. Do you know that a murder was committed because of you?"

"No, no!" cried Monks. "I knew nothing of that. I only heard about a murder, but I thought it was because of a common quarrel."

"No! It was done because the girl told part of your secret. Are you prepared to tell me the rest now?"

"Yes, I will."

"Will you sign a statement of the truth and repeat it in front of witnesses?"

"Yes, I'll do that too," said Monks.

"You must do even more. You remember what the will said. You must give your poor innocent brother, who has suffered so much, what is rightfully due him. Once that is done, you may go where you please. I won't send the law after you. I am interested only in Oliver's well-being. Then, I hope never to see you again."

"A Murder Was Committed Because of You."

Monks began angrily pacing the room, hoping to come up with a way to escape. Suddenly, Dr. Losberne burst in, violently upset.

"The murderer will be captured tonight!" he announced. "His dog has been seen lurking around an old haunt. Surely the man will go there under cover of darkness. There are policemen and spies everywhere, and the government has offered a reward of 100 pounds for his capture!"

"And what of Fagin?" asked Mr. Brownlow.

"Not taken yet, but he will be. They're sure of that. Harry Maylie is helping the police now."

Turning to Monks, Mr. Brownlow said, "This should convince you that you cannot get away, Edward Leeford. Stay here. It's the only place where you'll be safe."

With those words, Mr. Brownlow and Dr. Losberne locked the door and hurried away.

"The Murderer Will Be Captured Tonight!"

Discussing Fagin's Capture

# CHAPTER 23

# Sikes's Last Stand

Near the Thames River, in one of the most wretched areas of London, was a place called Jacob's Island. It was surrounded by a muddy ditch 20 feet wide. When the tide came in, it was filled with water 6 or 8 feet deep. In a decaying old house overlooking this ditch sat Toby Crackit and Charley Bates.

"When did they capture Fagin?" asked Toby.

"Just this afternoon," Charley replied. "I escaped up the chimney. Noah got into the big empty water cask, head-first, but his legs stuck out so far that he was seen and captured too. Even The Cripples isn't safe any-more. Everyone was taken into custody. But you should have seen Fagin! He went down fighting, all muddy and bleeding."

Suddenly, a pattering noise was heard on the stairs outside, and Bill Sikes's dog bounded into the room through an open win-dow. He was limping and almost dead from hunger and thirst.

"What's the meaning of this?" cried Toby. "I hope Sikes isn't coming here."

"He's probably out of the country by now."

Both agreed that this was probably so. They gave the dog some water and sat quietly as the hours passed.

Much later, the door burst open and Sikes entered, his face white, his eyes sunken. Toby and Charley gasped.

"Monster! Murderer!" shouted the men who had once been his friends in crime.

Their shouts were drowned out by the sounds of people and horses approaching the

Sikes Bursts In.

house.

"Twenty guineas to the man who brings a ladder!" shouted Harry Maylie's voice from the angry mob surrounding the house.

"The tide was in as I came up," cried Sikes. "Bring me a long rope. I'll climb up to the roof of the house and lower myself into the ditch! Give me a rope or I'll kill you."

Sikes climbed up to the roof and fastened one end of the rope tightly around the chimney. With the other end of the rope, he made a loop. He would lower himself with the rope, then cut it with his knife when he was almost touching the ground.

As he put the loop over his head and prepared to slip it under his armpits, Sikes lost his balance and tumbled off the roof. As he fell 35 feet, the noose got tighter and tighter around his neck. There was a sudden jerk, and the murderer hung lifeless against the wall of the house. The knife was still clenched in his stiffening hand.

Sikes Tries to Escape.

Oliver Recognizes Monks.

# CHAPTER 24

# Filling In the Missing Pieces

Oliver was back in the town of his birth. He had come there with Mrs. Maylie, Rose, Dr. Losberne, Mrs. Bedwin, Mr. Brownlow, Mr. Grimwig, and a young man whose name he didn't know. But it was the same man who had cursed at him when he went to post the letter to the doctor and the same man who had peered in at him as he sat on the porch of the Maylies' cottage.

When they were all seated in the big hotel room Mr. Brownlow had rented, Mr. Brownlow turned to Monks and, pointing at Oliver, he said, "This child is your half-brother, the son of your father and of Agnes Fleming—the young woman he had hoped to marry before his death. She died in giving birth to Oliver. Now, Monks, we must hear the rest of the story from you."

Monks was angry and sullen, but knew he had to tell his story to all the witnesses.

"Listen then!" he began. "My father—also Oliver's father—became ill in Rome. My mother and I joined him there. They had been living apart for a long time. After he died, I found two papers in his desk. One was a letter written to you, Mr. Brownlow, and the other was a letter to Agnes. She was carrying the unborn child then. He told her that he would marry her and hide her shame. He reminded her of the gifts of love he had given her—the ring and the little gold locket with her Christian name engraved on it and a blank space left for his name, which he hoped to add one day. He begged her to wear the locket next to her heart. . . ."

Monks Tells His Story to Witnesses.

As Oliver listened, tears streamed down his face.

"That's enough, Monks!" interrupted Mr. Brownlow. "Now, tell us about the will."

Monks was silent.

"*I'll* tell about it, then," said Mr. Brownlow. "It spoke of your father's unhappy marriage to your mother—a woman whose evil nature taught you, his only son, to hate him. You developed that same evil nature too. Yet in spite of that, your father left you and your mother each a yearly sum of 800 pounds in his will. Most of his property was left for Agnes Fleming and for their child. If the child were a boy, he would get his inheritance only if he never dishonored his name by breaking the law. This is why Monks conspired with Fagin to make the boy a criminal and one day have him get caught."

"My mother burned the will!" said Monks. "The letter never reached Agnes, but she told her father the truth about her unborn baby.

Oliver Weeps for His Mother.

Mr. Fleming fled with his two daughters to Wales. Because of his shame, he changed his name. But Agnes was too ashamed to stay, so she ran away and had her baby in the work-house of this town. Her father searched for her in vain. He was so sure she had killed herself that he died of a broken heart."

Mr. Brownlow took up the story:

"Years later, when Monks was 18, he ran away from home. His mother came to me for help. He had robbed her of money and jewelry, he had gambled, he had forged checks, and he had finally fled to London, where he made friends with the lowest char-acters. When his mother knew she was dying, she started a search for him. He was found, and he returned to France with her."

"Before she died," Monks broke in, "she re-vealed these secrets to me. She believed that a baby boy had been born to Agnes. I swore to her that if that child ever crossed my path, I would hunt him down, never let him rest, and

Agnes Fleming Ran Away in Shame.

show him my deepest hate. And I found that child. If I could, I would drag him to the gallows!"

Everyone gasped at this villain's words.

Mr. Brownlow then told his listeners that Monks gave Fagin a large reward for keeping Oliver trapped, but that Fagin would have to give up some part of it if the boy were rescued. A fight over this led them both to the country house to identify Oliver. That's when Oliver saw them, but they escaped.

"And now," said Mr. Brownlow, turning to Monks, "what about the locket and ring?"

"I bought them from the man and woman I told you about. They got the pawn ticket from the nurse who stole the gold from Agnes Fleming's dead body. You know where the locket and ring are now—at the bottom of the river."

Mr. Brownlow nodded to Mr. Grimwig, who went to the door and brought Mr. and Mrs. Bumble into the room. At first, they denied

Identifying Oliver

knowing anything about the locket and ring. Then Mr. Grimwig led two toothless old hags into the room.

"You shut the door the night Old Sally died," said the first one to Mrs. Bumble. "But we heard what she said."

Then the other old hag added, "We heard Old Sally try to tell you what she had done. Then we peeked in and saw you take a paper from her hand, and we followed you to the pawnbroker. And we saw you get the locket and gold ring."

"Would you like to see the pawnbroker himself?" Mr. Grimwig asked Mrs. Bumble.

"No," she answered. "I *did* sell the locket and ring. And if *he*"—and she pointed to Monks—"if he has been a coward and confessed, I have nothing more to say. I did sell them. . .to him!"

"I shall see to it that you and your husband never hold a position of trust again," said Mr. Brownlow. "You may go."

The Old Hags Accuse Mrs. Bumble.

After the Bumbles had gone, Mr. Brownlow turned to Rose. "Do not tremble, my dear. You need not fear my next few words."

Then, turning to Monks, he asked, "Do you know this young lady?"

"Yes," replied Monks.

"I never saw you before," said Rose in amazement.

"Agnes's father had *two* daughters," said Mr. Brownlow. "What happened to the other child, Monks?"

"When her father died in a strange place and with a strange name, no one was able to trace any relatives or friends for the young girl. So she was taken in and raised by some poor cottage people, but my mother found her and tormented her until her life was miserable. But one day, a widow lady living alone in the countryside saw the girl and took pity on her. She took the girl home to live with her and gave her a happy life. I didn't see the girl until a few months ago."

"Agnes's Father Had *Two* Daughters!"

"Where is she now?"

"Right in this room!" said Monks, pointing at Rose.

"Oh, my dear niece," cried Mrs. Maylie as Rose collapsed in her arms.

"My dear, darling aunt!" cried Oliver, rushing to hug Rose. The two orphans wept in each other's arms.

Just then, Harry Maylie entered the room.

"Dear Rose," he said, "I know everything. And I'm here to remind you of a promise you made to me."

"Now that you know all about my past," she cried, "I am even more unworthy of you than before."

"No," said the handsome young man. "I decided that if my world could not be yours, I would make your world mine. My important relatives and friends look down on me now, but I want nothing of their power and way of life. I want only to marry you, Rose, in a little country church!"

"My Dear, Darling Aunt!"

Guilty!

# CHAPTER 25

## One Last Glance

Fagin stood before the judge and jury in the crowded courtroom. The verdict was brought in to the breathless villagers— Guilty! Shouts of joy went up inside the courtroom and outside. He would die on the gallows Monday—in three days time.

When Oliver heard the news of Fagin's hanging, he said a quiet prayer for the old man.

Rose Fleming and Harry Maylie were married in the country church and enjoyed many years of happiness together, with all of Mrs. Maylie's blessings.

Mr. Brownlow arranged for the property of Oliver's father to be divided between Oliver and Monks. However, Monks squandered his share and soon returned to a life of crime. He died in a faraway jail.

The other members of Fagin's gang also met unhappy endings. Only Charley Bates escaped from a life of evil and became a respectable citizen. Noah Claypole had helped the police capture Fagin, so he received a pardon and remained free. But he never amounted to much in the world.

Mr. and Mrs. Bumble lost their positions as heads of the workhouse and became so poor and miserable that they had to live as paupers in the very same workhouse where they had once treated the orphans so badly.

As for Oliver himself, he became Mr. Brownlow's adopted son and put his old life behind him forever. If Agnes Fleming could have looked down on him from Heaven, she would have been very proud of her son.

Proud of Oliver

# ILLUSTRATED CLASSIC EDITIONS

MOBY BOOKS

AC-B4500-2/58